40

S0-CCJ-724

KIDNAP!

Lisa Eisenberg

A PACEMAKER® BOOK

FEARON EDUCATION, A DIVISION OF
PITMAN LEARNING, INC.
BELMONT, CALIFORNIA

South City Cops™ Series

> Break-In
>
> Hit Man
>
> **Kidnap!**
>
> Murder Behind the Wheel
>
> On the Run
>
> The Payoff Game

Cover photographer: Richard Hutchings

Copyright © 1984 by Pitman Learning, Inc.,
19 Davis Drive, Belmont, California 94002.
Member of the Pitman Group. All rights reserved.
No part of this book may be reproduced by
any means, transmitted, or translated into a
machine language without written permission
from the publisher.

ISBN-0-8224-6263-X
Library of Congress Catalog Card Number: 83-63333
Printed in the United States of America.
1. 9 8 7 6 5 4 3 2 1

Contents

1 **Kids and Parades**

MAY 3, 11:30 A.M.

The children were running around in the bright spring sunshine on the grassy playground. Every now and then, one of them would skip over to the nursery school teacher by the door. The teacher would nod or smile and say something to the child. Then the child would return to the others and begin playing again.

No one noticed the tall, thin, blond man outside the school gate. He was pretending to fix something under the hood of an old black car parked on the street. But he really was studying the playground. Watching for one special child. Waiting for him to show up.

At last, he was sure he saw him. The little boy's blond hair shone in the sun. He was playing in the center of a group of children. Suddenly he ran to one of the others and tapped her shoulder. The girl skipped into the middle, and the blond boy took her place in the circle.

The tall man slipped around to the other side of the black car. He reached into his pocket and pulled out an old photo. The picture showed the face of a smiling blond boy.

"That's him all right," the man whispered to himself. "And tomorrow's the day when I start taking care of him. Like I should."

Just then, a few cars pulled up on the street. The parents were coming to pick up their children. The teacher waved good-bye to each boy and girl. The children went off to their homes.

A long, shiny, silver sedan came for the little blond boy. He waved to his friends, hugged his teacher, and ran toward the car. Then he jumped into the back seat.

The tall, thin man watched the sedan as it headed back up the street and around the corner. "Tomorrow," he whispered again. "Tomorrow's the day."

MAY 4, 7:30 A.M.

Kate Brightwater and Eddy Hall were tired. They had been up late the night before finishing the paperwork on their last case. Now they were sitting around, waiting for a new assignment.

Kate called her father to remind him about his appointment with the doctor that morning. Jason Brightwater, who lived with his daughter, was ill. He and Kate had moved from the country so he could be treated at South City Hospital. Kate wanted to make sure he didn't forget to go for his weekly hospital visit.

Kate hung up the phone. Eddy watched her brew some homemade sage tea at her desk. He made some gagging noises in his throat. But Brightwater didn't look up. Finally he said, "How can you drink that stuff? Just looking at it makes me sick!"

Kate's brown eyes didn't even glance his

way. "Leave me alone, Hall. Go drown yourself in that wonderful mud you drink from the coffee shop downstairs."

Eddy shook his head and turned away. He wandered over toward a young cop named Skip. He placed his large body on the edge of Skip's desk.

"How are you guys doing on that escaped convict case?" he asked. "The one that broke out of Quincy Prison."

Skip shook his head. "You must mean Slippery Jay," he said. "We're not getting anywhere. We've checked out every place he might have gone. But there hasn't been any sign of him. I guess he didn't get nicknamed Slippery for nothing."

Eddy smiled and patted Skip's arm. "You'll get him, kid," he said. But as Eddy walked back to his own desk, he wasn't so sure. He wished he and Brightwater could get assigned to that case. The idea of people escaping from jail and walking the streets didn't make him happy. And Eddy Hall had always been good at tracking people down. He had a way of putting himself in their shoes, thinking the way they would think.

But Precinct Captain Steele was planning

something very different for Kate and Eddy. The captain was staring at a small TV on his desk. The TV showed a group of people marching downtown.

"Who've we got on crowd control, Wilkins?" the captain asked.

Sergeant Wilkins checked his list. "Let's see," he said. "There's Tucker and Jackson, Lopez and Coletti."

Captain Steele brushed the crumbs from his breakfast off his desk. "I don't want any trouble down there," he said. "Put some more people on it. How about Hall and Brightwater? They're free now, aren't they?"

"As of last night, yes, they are."

The captain looked at the people on TV. "What are those nuts doing down there, anyway?" he growled. "Marching around town at this hour of the morning. It shouldn't be allowed. What in the world are they marching about?"

Sergeant Wilkins turned away to hide a smile. "It's a Help Your Local Police march, Captain. The mayor and all the other precinct captains are marching, too, to show support. Some are even making speeches."

Captain Steele was on his feet. "What?" he

cried. His round face was getting red. "Why wasn't I told about this?"

Sergeant Wilkins groaned inside. He had only himself to blame. He should have made sure the captain was listening yesterday afternoon when he had told him about the march. He had told the captain five times during the past week. But that was no excuse.

The captain was yanking his jacket over his full stomach. "There's still time to get down there before anyone misses me," he said. "Order me a car. On the double, Wilkins!"

The sergeant left the captain's office and called over to a cop named Sylvia. She ran off to get the captain's car. A few minutes later, Captain Steele hurried out the door and down the steps to the street.

Sergeant Wilkins braced himself and put on his best smile. He looked over at Hall and Brightwater. He didn't like what he saw. They looked in no mood to hear what he had to tell them.

Quickly he crossed the room toward their desks. He had better get it over with. But he knew one thing. Kate and Eddy weren't going to like hearing that they had been stuck with crowd control duty that morning. Still, there was nothing to do but give them the bad news.

A moment later, the two cops were fighting on their way to their car in the police parking lot. "I wish he'd put us on that Slippery Jay case," Hall growled. "Who needs crowd control?"

"I don't like it any better than you do, Hall!" snapped Kate. "But if you're going to complain all day, you can walk!"

Without another word, Hall and Brightwater climbed into the car. Kate started the engine. Then they followed Captain Steele's car through the streets to downtown.

2 **A New Driver**

MAY 4, 8:00 A.M.

Rolfie Lundquist was playing on the sidewalk in front of his house. He played there almost every morning when it wasn't raining. He knew he was supposed to stay right in front of the steps. And he knew someone from inside the house would check on him every few minutes.

Rolfie bounced his orange ball against the brick building. Then he drew some pictures on the sidewalk with his chalk. The spring air felt warm and good. The little boy's blond hair looked almost white in the sunshine.

Rolfie was waiting to go to nursery school. He wished it was time to go. He loved school and could hardly wait to get there each morning.

After a few minutes, Rolfie looked up from his game. A long, silver sedan was pulling up in front of the house. The little boy ran out to the edge of the curb. There he stopped short. Someone new was driving the family car.

The driver opened his door and stepped out of the car. "Hi there, kiddo. Come on. Hop in back. It's time to go to school."

Rolfie stood still and stared. "But . . . who are you?" he asked.

The driver looked surprised. "Didn't your mom and dad tell you? I'm their old friend, Mr. Jay. I'm filling in for the regular guy today. He's sick." He tapped his black uniform. "See? He let me wear his clothes. And he gave me the car keys."

The man walked around the car toward the boy. He opened the back door and told him to get in. As Rolfie started climbing in, a voice called out, "Hi, Rolfie!"

Rolfie looked back and saw a neighbor, Mrs. Finney, walking her dog, Giant.

"Hi!" he called over his shoulder. "I'm going to nursery school."

The driver tipped his black cap at the neighbor. Then he hurried around to the front seat. Quickly, he started the engine and took off down the street. The tires squealed as he went around the corner.

Mrs. Finney watched the car speed away. "That's strange, Giant," she said to her dog. "The Lundquists have hired another new driver. He seems polite. But I wonder if they know how fast he drives that big car of theirs!"

MAY 4, 9:00 A.M.

Hall and Brightwater had been assigned to regular patrol duty that morning. As they drove up and down the South City streets, Hall complained about being bored.

"At least it's not crowd control again." Kate smiled. "Wasn't that terrible yesterday? Who would have thought police supporters could be so wild?" Today she was able to joke about it. She had slept well. And her father was feeling better after his treatment at the hospital.

But Eddy still wasn't happy. "I wish Steele would put me on that escaped convict case," he said for the fifth time. "I have a feeling I could find that guy. Skip let me read the file yesterday and . . . "

"Stop talking about it, Hall. We're not on the case, and that's that. The captain can't have the whole department running after one man. There are plenty of crimes in South City. He's probably saving us for one of those."

Just as Brightwater finished speaking, a call came in on the radio. "Missing child reported," a voice said. "At Six Blueberry Square. Please respond if you are in the area."

At once, Kate reached for the radio. "Car ninety-four in the area of Blueberry Square," she said. "We're responding right away."

Eddy swung the car around in the middle of the busy street. The driver behind them had to slam on her brakes. Hall stepped on the gas.

Eddy and Kate weren't sure yet if this call

would turn into a real case. Most missing children turned up playing next door or hiding under their beds. But still, speed was important. By getting to the scene fast, they could start a search before the child got too far away.

Kate and Eddy reached Blueberry Square quickly. The houses there were big and fancy. As the car pulled up in front of number 6, Eddy's eyes opened wide.

"Say! I've been here before. This house belonged to a doctor—a man named Lundquist. He was a really nice guy."

Eddy looked down at his hands. "My wife Ava and I came here to see if he could help her. She had been sick for so long. Must have been about three years ago. Right before she died."

Eddy looked up at the house again. "I wonder if Dr. Lundquist still lives here," he said. "It's funny. I don't remember them having a child. But of course, he might not have said anything about it."

The two police officers left the car and started toward 6 Blueberry Square. It was a beautiful old house that was almost the size of a mansion. The houses up and down the street were much the same.

The two police officers stopped when they came to the bottom of some carved stone steps. Loud, angry voices were coming from an open front window. Kate and Eddy stared at each other. They both listened hard.

"You did *what*, Tina?" demanded a loud male voice.

A woman's shaky voice answered, "I called the police, sir. I looked out, and Rolfie was gone! I called and hunted everywhere, but I couldn't find him. You and Dr. Ingrid weren't around, so I felt I had to call the police!"

Another woman's voice joined in. "Oh, how could you, Tina? We've told you our story. You know how we feel about the police. What's going to happen now?"

The voices got softer as the people moved away from the window. Hall and Brightwater looked at each other. They were both thinking the same thing. What possible reason could the Lundquists have for not wanting the police called in?

They climbed the steps as fast as they could. Eddy pressed the doorbell and held his finger there. They were in no mood to wait around. They wanted answers from the Lundquist family—fast.

3 Questions

MAY 4, 9:10 A.M.

Rolfie didn't understand why it was taking so long to get to nursery school. They had been driving and driving. But nothing he saw out the window looked anything like his school.

At last, the driver pulled into a parking lot off a busy street. He stopped by a low, flat building with a lot of doors and numbers. He came around and opened Rolfie's door.

"Come on out, kiddo."

"But . . . where are we? This isn't my school."

The tall, thin, blond man put a strong hand on Rolfie's arm. The little boy felt himself being lifted out of the car and held in the air.

"I forgot to tell you," said the man. "Your school's closed for the day. You get to spend the morning here."

Rolfie's feet never touched the ground. The man carried him under one arm. With his free hand he unlocked a door with a number 2 on it. Inside, he put Rolfie down and locked the door again.

The little boy looked around at a small room with one large bed. The place was dark and too warm. Rolfie didn't like it at all.

"What am I going to do here?" he asked.

"Wait for your mom to come and get you, kiddo. And you're going to sit still. And keep real quiet."

Rolfie spotted a large TV in one corner. He ran over and turned the set on loud.

The blond man moved quickly. He reached behind the TV and jerked out a wire. The screen went black.

Rolfie blinked in surprise. "Sorry, kid," the man said. "They don't want any noise here. No TV allowed."

The boy looked so sad, the man couldn't help giving him a rough pat on the head. Rolfie jumped back. The man sighed. "Oh, well," he thought. "He'll get to know me. Soon we'll have all the time in the world."

MAY 4, 9:15 A.M.

Hall and Brightwater were in the large living room of Doctors Lars and Ingrid Lundquist. The maid, Tina, was there, too. She was crying softly and wiping her eyes with the corner of her apron.

Both police officers had their notebooks and pens out. They wanted to write down some information about where Rolfie had been that morning. But so far, there hadn't been a lot to write down. The Lundquists seemed nervous when the officers asked them about their child.

"I sent him outside," Tina said for the third time. "The way I do every morning. Just to play for a few minutes. I always check on him often. But today, when I looked out . . . he was gone! At first, I didn't worry. I thought he'd just come inside for a minute. But then I

searched the house. And up and down the
street. And I called him and called him.
And . . . "

"Calm down, Tina," broke in Lars Lundquist. "I'm sure Rolfie will turn up somewhere soon. You shouldn't always get so upset
about everything."

Eddy tried not to let the surprise show on
his face. This was the same Dr. Lars Lundquist who had treated his wife three years ago.
But he seemed like a different man. Of course,
any father would be worried about his missing
child. But this man wasn't acting worried. He
almost seemed to be hiding something.

His wife was acting the same way. "I'm
sure we don't need to have the police in the
house," she said. "You made a mistake,
Tina."

Tina started to say something angry, but
she seemed to change her mind. She shook her
head and started crying again. Clearly, she still
thought she had done the right thing.

Eddy tried again. "What is the boy's usual
schedule in the morning?" he asked.

"He gets up early and eats breakfast. One of
us helps him get dressed, and then he plays

for a while," said Ingrid Lundquist. "A little before nine, our chauffeur takes him to nursery school—the Little Acorn School over on Oak Way."

"But no one's seen him since eight this morning?" Kate asked.

"Well . . . no," said Ingrid. She tried to sound calm, but her hands in her lap were shaking. "But I'm sure he's just off playing somewhere. I expect him to walk through the door any minute!"

"He's never done this before," Tina muttered.

Kate and Eddy closed their notebooks and stood up. "I think we need to check around the house again," said Kate. "And the neighborhood. We'll talk to the neighbors and the chauffeur. Let's hope Rolfie is just around the corner."

As she and Hall stepped out the front door, they whispered a few words to each other. "What's going on in there with these people?" Eddy hissed. "It's as if they don't want us to find the little boy."

"I know," Kate whispered back. "The maid, Tina, is the only one who wants us around. They all are acting worried about something—something besides the missing child."

They walked down the steps to the street and studied the neighbors' houses. Just then, a woman with a dog came around the corner. Her eyes opened wide as she saw the police car. She hurried up to them.

"Is something wrong?" she asked. "I live right here—in number eight."

"We're looking for the little boy from number six," explained Kate. "Rolfie Lundquist. His family noticed he was missing around eight. Have you seen him by any chance?"

"Why, yes, I did," the woman said. "He told me he was going to school."

Kate quickly wrote down the woman's name and address—*Mrs. Finney, 8 Blueberry Square.* "Tell me, ma'am. About what time did you see Rolfie?"

"A little after eight," Mrs. Finney answered. "I was just on my way to the park with Giant here. Come to think of it, it did seem a little early for Rolfie to be going off. Usually when Giant and I go for a walk, Rolfie is still playing around outside."

Kate and Eddy gave each other a quick look. "Who took the boy, Mrs. Finney?" they both asked at once. "How did he go?" Eddy added.

"In the Lundquists' car, of course. The big silver one. Their new chauffeur was driving. A nice-looking man. And very polite. He even tipped his hat at me. But my goodness, was he ever driving fast!"

4 An Old Picture

MAY 4, 10:00 A.M.

Rolfie sat on the bed in the room marked number 2. The tall, thin, blond man was trying to read a newspaper. But the boy's crying was getting on his nerves.

"Listen, kiddo," he said at last. "You've got to stop all that noise. I told you they don't like noise here."

The little boy's cries got louder. "But I want Mommy," he said. "And Daddy. And Tina."

The man got to his feet. "Soon, I told you. They'll be here soon. You don't want them to find you sitting around crying like a baby, do you?"

Rolfie cried even louder. The blond man made up his mind. He had planned to wait until later. But someone was sure to hear the crying before long. The walls in this dump were as thin as paper.

"Listen, are you as hungry as I am, kiddo?" he asked. "There's a food machine just outside. I'll be right back."

Before Rolfie could speak, the man left the room and walked to some machines with candy and drinks nearby. Minutes later, he was back with his hands full.

"Look! Chocolate milk and peanut butter crackers!"

Rolfie sniffed and sat up straight. With a shaking hand, he reached out for the snack. The man handed him the crackers. But he took the milk into the bathroom.

"I'll find a glass," he called to the boy. "Can't have you drinking right out of the carton."

Inside the bathroom, he put down the milk. He felt in his pocket for a tiny white envelope. Swiftly he tapped out some white powder into the bottom of a water glass. Then he opened the chocolate milk and poured it into the same glass. He shook it gently to be sure the powder was mixed in. Then he went back out to the boy.

"Here you go, kiddo! I'll bet you like this stuff."

Rolfie had already eaten two peanut butter crackers. He was feeling thirsty. He reached for the glass and took several long drinks. Then halfway through, he made a face. "It tastes funny," he said.

"Go on. It's OK," the man said in a nervous voice. "Drink it up."

But Rolfie had put the milk down. He started to bite another cracker. But all at once, he stopped.

"I don't feel very good," he said in a quiet voice.

"You better lie down then, sonny. Right on the bed there. Just put your feet up and . . . "

The tall, thin man stopped talking. The little boy had already curled up and fallen into a deep, drugged sleep.

MAY 4, 10:15 A.M.

Kate and Eddy went back into the Lundquist home. They needed to check with Rolfie's nursery school to see if he had turned up.

Perhaps the new chauffeur had gotten mixed up and had taken the boy in early. But when they called the Little Acorn School, no one had seen or heard from the Lundquist child. The teachers had been about to call his house to see if he was sick.

The maid, Tina, was standing right behind Kate when she put down the phone. Her eyes were dry now, but she still looked worried.

"He's not at the school?" she asked.

"No, I'm afraid not, Tina," Kate answered. She lowered her voice. "Listen. Have both of Rolfie's parents been in all morning?" She and Eddy were still trying to figure out why the Lundquists were acting so strange.

The maid twisted her hands. "Well, I couldn't find them when I first noticed that Rolfie was missing. But then I found them in their office where they see patients. They were going over some files. I'm sure they hadn't gone out anywhere. Toby would have noticed if they took one of the cars."

Eddy stared at her. "Toby? Who's that?"

"Why the new driver, of course. You sent me to look for him, but I guess I never told you his name. He lives in an apartment over the garage. I don't think he's there. I just called him on the house phone. There was no answer."

Kate and Eddy had already checked the bottom part of the garage where the car was kept. They had found the door closed and the garage empty. But they hadn't known anything about an upstairs apartment.

"Maybe you better take us up to his room, Tina," Kate said. "Doesn't he usually tell you when he's going out?"

"Well, he's supposed to," the maid said. She led them outside in back of the house.

Kate whispered to her partner. "The neighbor said the chauffeur took Rolfie off to school. But he never turned up there. If both he and the Lundquists' car are gone . . ."

"I know what you mean," Eddy said softly. "We need to find out some more about this guy Toby."

The tiny apartment was so neat and clean that it was hard to believe anyone really lived there. There was no sign of Toby.

Eddy went to the front of the room overlooking the street. He found a pair of binoculars right by an open window.

"Looks like our friend Toby is interested in

watching birds," he said. "Or watching something out there, anyway."

Kate poked through the closet and checked under the bed. Then she looked through a pile of papers on a desk in the corner. Finally she saw something sticking out from under the corner of the desk blotter. She pulled out a picture of a little blond boy.

"Say, Tina," she called to the maid, who was watching them from the doorway. "Who's this little boy?"

The maid came forward and stared at the picture. "Why . . . where in the world did Toby get that?" she asked out loud. "It's a picture of Rolfie. But it's not a new picture. He looks quite a bit older now. Why that must have been taken just about the time when he was . . ." The maid suddenly stopped talking in the middle of her sentence.

Eddy crossed the room and looked at the picture. He turned it around and saw some writing on the back.

"Ralphie Judson," he read slowly. Tina gasped, and he gave her a sharp look. "Now who in the world is that?" he asked the maid in a hard voice.

Tina turned red, then white. "I . . . I don't know what that name is doing on there," she said. "It must be some mistake!"

"I think there have been a lot of mistakes around here this morning!" Eddy snapped. "The main one is that you and the Lundquists have been lying to us."

"I think we better go back to the house and have another meeting with the Lundquists," Kate said. "We can't do anything until we have the real story."

Hall and Brightwater didn't speak as they followed the maid down the stairs and back around to the main house. Their faces looked angry.

"Please tell the Lundquists that we want to meet with them," Eddy said to Tina. "Down here in the living room. Now!"

5 The Phone Call

The tall, thin, blond man watched the little boy sleeping on the bed. He lay very still. Only the quiet sound of his breathing showed he was still alive.

The man wished the boy had drunk all the drugged chocolate milk. Still, he seemed to be out cold. And even if he woke up, he couldn't go anywhere.

The kidnapper felt in his jacket pocket. His fingers touched the cold metal of his gun. It made him feel safer, stronger somehow. As if he really was in control of the world.

With a last look at the boy, the man decided to leave the room. His eyes came to rest on the telephone on the corner table. He couldn't risk using it. And he didn't want the boy picking it up either.

Quickly the man crossed the room and pulled the phone wire from the wall. He was doing a lot of damage to this place. But by the time the motel manager found out, he and the kid would be long gone.

The man left the room and checked to be sure the door was locked. He knew the boy wouldn't be able to get out. The bolt was too high for the little kid to reach. Then the man walked to a nearby gas station. He entered a phone booth and closed the door.

He had learned the number by heart. As he dialed, he was glad to see how steady his hands were. So far, this job was going along as smooth as silk.

A worried male voice answered the phone on the first ring. There was a slight click right after that. Someone else had picked up another phone in the house. That was all right. Let the police listen in. There was nothing they could do to stop him. Not as long as he had the boy.

"Hello? Who's there?" said the voice. "This is Doctor Lars Lundquist speaking."

The kidnapper slipped a cloth over the mouthpiece of the phone. "I've got the boy," he whispered.

Dr. Lundquist took a sharp breath. "Who is this? How do I know you're telling the truth? How do I know you have my child?"

"*Your* child! What a joke. But that's not the point. The point is, you better believe me if you want the kid safe. Do you want to know what to do or not?"

"Yes, yes. Tell us what you want. Please!"

"That's more like it. Now here's what you do. Put fifty thousand dollars in a plain brown bag. Go to Fifth and Franklin tonight at eight. There's a phone booth on the southwest corner. Leave the money there. Bring it yourself, Lundquist. No cops with you. You got all that?"

"Wait . . . wait. Could you tell me all that again? I . . . I missed part of it."

"You heard me, pal. Don't try to keep me

talking. It won't do you any good. Just bring the money yourself. Tonight."

"But . . . "

The man in the phone booth had already put down the phone and had left the gas station.

MAY 4, 10:45 A.M.

Hall and Brightwater had been listening in on the phone in the living room. They rushed into the library, where Lars and Ingrid Lundquist were sitting. Both husband and wife had tears in their eyes.

"All right!" Kate snapped. "You can't pretend nothing has happened now. What did the kidnapper mean on the phone when he said it was a joke about Rolfie being *your* boy?"

Lars Lundquist was too choked up to speak. His wife turned her worried face toward the police officers.

"It's . . . it's true," she whispered. "We think of Rolfie as ours . . . but he wasn't always ours. We adopted him when he was a very small boy."

Dr. Lars pulled himself together. "You see . . . his parents were criminals. His mother was killed trying to hold up a bank. His father was caught during the robbery. He was tried and sent to jail upstate."

"So that's why you've been acting so funny all morning!" broke in Eddy. "You haven't told Rolfie he's adopted. And you were afraid that somehow the truth about his parents would come out once the police started snooping around."

"Yes, you're right," said Ingrid. "I'm sorry. I know we were wrong. I only hope we haven't made things worse for Rolfie by trying to hide the truth."

Kate took Eddy's arm and pulled him out into the front hall. "We have to call in the FBI now that we know we have a kidnapping on our hands," she said. "Kidnapping is a federal crime."

"I know," said Eddy. "But something has been bothering me." He felt in his pocket. "Where's that picture of the boy? The one we found up in the chauffeur's room. Something about it has been on my mind . . ."

Kate pulled the photograph out of her own

shirt pocket. Eddy took it and read the back. "Ralphie Judson," he said slowly. Suddenly he slapped a large hand against his forehead. "That's it!" he shouted. "Slippery Jay!"

"What are you talking about, Hall?" Kate asked. "Have you gone out of your mind?"

"Slippery Jay!" her partner cried again. "That escaped con everyone's been hunting for. If I'm not wrong, his last name is Judson. Remember, Skip let me read the file on the case. I think Judson is Jay's real name. And he was in Quincy Prison for armed robbery!"

Kate sat down hard on a step. "Wow," she said. "You mean Rolfie Lundquist is Ralphie Judson—Slippery Judson's son. But why would Judson kidnap his own child? He's an escaped con. Does he think he can bring the child up while he's on the run?"

"I don't know. But it's interesting, isn't it? Judson escapes, and two weeks later his boy is kidnapped. Hard to believe it's all just chance."

"It's also hard to believe that the Lundquists' chauffeur isn't behind all this," Kate said slowly. "The neighbor says she saw him drive off with Rolfie at eight. And neither one of them has been seen since."

Just then, the maid came through the hall on her way to the kitchen. Kate and Eddy stopped her.

"Tina," Kate said, "what else can you tell us about the new chauffeur, Toby? Do you know him very well?"

"Oh, no, Officer Brightwater. He's only been working here about a week and a half. And he keeps to himself all the time. Rolfie loves him, though. Hangs around him quite a bit."

"Oh," said Kate. "Well, what does Toby look like?"

"Sort of tall . . . thin . . . light hair. Not very unusual."

"How did he get the job?" Eddy asked. "Did anyone check up on his background?"

Tina looked uncomfortable. "Well, he had letters from people he'd worked for before. But I'm not sure anyone checked them out. Probably the Lundquists should have been more careful. But he knew how to handle that big car so well. Doctor Lars hired him on the spot."

Hall and Brightwater let Tina go on with her work. Then they turned to look at each other.

"Are you thinking what I'm thinking?" Eddy asked his partner.

"I think I am," she answered. "It's beginning to look like the <u>Lundquists</u> hired an escaped convict to be their chauffeur. A convict named <u>Slippery Jay Judson</u>—the man who is the father of their adopted child."

6 Slippery Jay

MAY 4, 11:00 A.M.

After making his phone call, the kidnapper
went back to the motel and checked on the
boy. Rolfie's breathing was still deep and
even. The drugged milk had really knocked
him out.

The tall man paced around the room for a
few minutes. Then he decided he could go
out to make his plans. He didn't want to go
back to the phone booth. He wasn't far from
the airport, so he decided to drive out there
and take care of things in person.

He pulled the curtains over the shades so

the room would be as dark as possible. Then he went outside, locked the door, and climbed into the car. He smiled as he got behind the wheel. He knew he was taking a chance driving the car around town. But being behind the wheel of a baby like this was fun.

Fifteen minutes later, the kidnapper parked in the airport lot. He walked to the Universal Airlines entrance and went inside. There he picked up a schedule and studied it. In minutes, he had made up his mind. He stepped to the counter.

"Any space left on the ten fifteen to L.A. tonight?"

The woman behind the counter checked her computer. "Yes," she said with a smile. "How many seats do you need for tonight?"

"Two. One adult. One child."

"And how do you plan to pay, Mr. . . . uh . . . "

"Jackson. My name is Jackson." The man cleared his throat. "Can I pay tonight? Before the flight takes off?"

"Certainly, Mr. Jackson. Come at least thirty minutes before the flight. You can pick up your tickets and pay for them then."

The kidnapper felt better with the seats reserved. He returned to the car and headed back to the motel. Rolfie was still sound asleep, flat on his stomach.

The man pulled a suitcase out from under the bed. He found a brown paper bag inside. He took it out and opened it. Then he picked up a copy of the *South City Times*. Slowly he began ripping it into small pieces and stuffing it into the bag. As he worked, he talked to the sleeping child.

"You won't understand any of this for a while, kiddo," he said. "But I'm doing it all for you. Someday I'll tell you how I bought a fresh start for both of us. Once you get over being scared of me, you'll understand. You'll thank me. Because after tonight, we're going to have everything we need in the whole wide world!"

MAY 4, 11:30 A.M.

Hall and Brightwater talked on the phone with the FBI for half an hour. They filled them in on the case. The FBI asked them to help out by staying on the job since they already had the inside track. Kate and Eddy were happy to hear that. Both of them wanted to help catch the kidnapper at the drop that night.

Kate had called the precinct house from the Lundquists' living room. She had given a description of the missing silver sedan. And she had said that she and Eddy would return to the station as soon as the FBI arrived.

After meeting with agents Darwin Stubbs and Harry Bruce at the house, the two police officers got back in their car and headed downtown. Without asking his partner, Eddy pulled into the parking lot of the Hot Dog Hangout. He jumped out and said, "I'm going to run in and pick up a couple of foot-long dogs with chili, cheese, and onions. What will you have?"

Kate gave him a cold stare. "I don't suppose they have a salad? Or a tofu plate?"

Eddy made a noise in his throat and shook his head. "You're kidding, of course," he said. "I'll surprise you with something you'll love."

Ten minutes later, he came back to the car. Kate slid over behind the wheel. "I'll drive while you eat," she said.

"But I got you something to eat. The healthiest thing they had. Fried onion rings."

Kate looked sick. "No, thanks," she said weakly. She started the car as Eddy bit into his first hot dog. "Besides, I couldn't eat anything anyway. Not even health food. I keep thinking about little Rolfie. He must be so scared by now."

"If he's still all right," said Eddy.

They finished the ride downtown in silence. Back at the police station, Kate reported to Captain Steele and Sergeant Wilkins. Eddy asked Skip if he could see the file on Slippery Jay Judson again.

After her report, Kate found Eddy at his desk. He was reading through the Slippery Jay file. "I was right," he told her. "Jay's real name is Judson. His wife was killed in the robbery that landed him in jail. And they had a small baby at the time. But that's not the worst of it."

"Oh? What else does it say in there?"

"That Judson's a real nut," said Eddy. "A hothead. He was always getting in trouble in Quincy. Fights with guards, other prisoners. In fact, he's been in trouble most of his life.

Also, he loves guns. Carries at least one wherever he goes. And likes to use it, too!"

"Oh, dear. That means that if he's got Rolfie, there's no telling what he'll do. We can only hope he wouldn't want to hurt his own child."

Kate looked at her notebook and found the Lundquists' phone number. "Now that we've got our hands on the description of Slippery Jay," she said, "we need a better one of Toby, the chauffeur. Maybe the computer can match up the descriptions and tell us if they're the same person."

A few minutes later, Kate hung up the phone. "The Lundquists don't have any pictures of Toby—whose last name is Thomas. But I read the description of Judson to them from the file. They said it sounds quite a bit like Toby. But there are a lot of tall, thin, blond men in the world."

Eddy sighed and sat back in his chair. "True," he said. "And we have no way of finding out if Toby is the right one. All we can do is wait till tonight."

"Right," said Kate. "If Toby Thomas shows up for the money, we'll know he and

Judson are one and the same. Let's hope that, by then, it won't be too late for Rolfie Lundquist."

7 The Drop

The kidnapper had gotten Rolfie back to sleep again. The boy had awakened in the late afternoon. He had cried and had looked scared. The man had fed him a hamburger from a nearby fast-food place. This time, he had slipped the drug into a vanilla milkshake. Once again, Rolfie had drunk only half of it. But he had gone right to sleep after dinner.

"Don't worry, kiddo," the kidnapper whispered as he left the room. "You'll understand all of this. Someday soon."

As the man climbed into the car, he put the bag full of torn newspaper on the seat beside him. He smiled as he thought about his clever plan. It hadn't been easy. But he had found a car that looked almost exactly like the Lundquists' silver sedan. It had already worked for him once. Rolfie's snoopy neighbor with the dog hadn't blinked an eye. She had watched the boy go off with him—a perfect stranger. But she had been fooled by the car.

And the car would fool the police tonight. He had told Lundquist to bring the $50,000 himself. But the FBI and police were sure to be watching the drop. After Lundquist dropped off the money in the phone booth and drove away in his silver sedan, he would drive up in this silver car. The police would think that Lundquist was returning for some reason. In the confusion, he would have a chance to swap his bag for the money. Drive away with it right under their noses. And if there was a foul-up, he could shoot his way out of trouble.

The silver sedan turned left onto Fifth Street. It was already starting to get dark. Good, the man thought. The darker the

better. The less likely the police would be to spot him—Ralphie Judson's father.

MAY 4, 8:00 P.M.

Hall and Brightwater had been sitting near the drop point for over an hour. They were parked across the street in a van with the words *Fred's Fancy Flowers* on the side of it.

Just around the corner, two FBI agents waited in a souped-up racing car. They were wearing T-shirts and jeans, trying to look like high school students. Other agents were stationed at points up and down the nearby streets.

Eddy had looked at the agents' outfits and laughed. "At least we get to wear uniforms," he had said. He and Kate were dressed in green outfits with *Fred's Flowers* printed on the back.

At exactly 8:00, a nervous Dr. Lars Lundquist drove up in his family's second car—a low, black convertible. Kate and Eddy had tried to talk him into letting an FBI agent come in his place.

"No!" the frightened father had said. "He

said it should be *me*. He might be watching.
He'll know."

"But it'll be dark," Kate had argued. "The
agent can dress like you and wear a wig.
Judson—or Toby—or whoever—won't be able
to tell. It'll be safer."

But Lundquist had insisted on coming himself. So, at 8:00, Kate and Eddy watched him
arrive. He parked the black car at the corner.
Then he got out and walked slowly to the
phone booth. Eddy thought he could see the
man's hands shaking from all the way across
the street.

Lundquist put the brown bag full of money
on the floor of the phone booth. Then he
returned to the car and drove away up Fifth
Street. He had followed the kidnapper's
instructions exactly.

"All we can do now is wait," Kate whispered to Eddy. "I wonder if he'll bring the
boy with him."

"I don't know. If it's Judson, remember
he's the boy's father. I hope I'm wrong.
But I have a feeling he might have some crazy
idea abut keeping the kid."

Kate looked sick. "And he's gun crazy, too,

you say. And . . . " She broke off. "Look, Hall! Isn't that the sedan—the Lundquists' other car—coming back up Fifth?"

The two police officers stared out the window of the van. In seconds, Eddy got on the radio and called the FBI car. They had seen the silver car coming and were watching it, too.

"It doesn't make sense," Eddy said. "Why is he being so bold? He must know we'd have the phone booth staked out. But he's driving up like he owns the place!"

All at once, Kate gunned the engine of the van. She pulled hard on the wheel and shot out into the middle of the street. The silver sedan had been slowing down, getting ready to park. But the driver must have sensed there was a trap. He sped up again and squealed north on Fifth. Kate jumped the corner and bounced after him. An oncoming car slammed on its brakes and blasted its horn.

Eddy grabbed the door handle and stared at his partner. "How could he have spotted us so fast?" he asked.

Kate didn't answer. She worked hard to follow the big silver car. It had just swerved onto a dark, narrow side street. Brightwater almost raced by it. Just in time, she made the turn.

"It's him," she said between her teeth. "I mean, it's a thin guy with blond hair. I saw him when our headlights hit his car and . . ."

She broke off as she zoomed around a car backing out of a driveway. The van went up on the curb and shot across a piece of lawn. The dark shape of a large oak sprang up in front of their faces. Eddy choked on a yell. Suddenly the van spun to the right, missing the tree by inches. They thumped back onto the road.

Kate acted as if nothing had happened. "I see his taillights up there," she said. "We're catching up to him."

Eddy stared through the darkness at the car ahead. They roared around another sharp turn. "I think he's heading for the highway," he told his partner.

All at once, the red taillights in front of them were gone.

"Oh, no!" Kate cried. "He's turned off his lights. It's now or never!"

She slammed the gas pedal down to the floor. But as the van leaped forward, they heard a loud sound. A huge moving truck had turned onto the street directly in front of them. There was no way to get by it. The van was heading straight for the side of the big truck.

Kate hit the brakes and jerked the wheel. Fred's Fancy Flowers van left the road once again and flew onto someone's lawn. They hit a patch of thick wet grass and swung around in two wide circles.

Crash! The van sailed over a huge bump. Suddenly they stopped. The front end of the van was tilted in the air.

At the same moment, they both opened their doors and jumped down to the ground. Eddy groaned loudly. The two front wheels of the van had gone over a low stone wall around a goldfish pond. They would never be able to get it out without a crane and a tow truck.

"What a mess," Eddy said. "Some driving, Brightwater!"

"Shut up, Hall," Kate said. "Who cares about my driving? The worst thing is that the kidnapper is long gone by now!"

"Well, at least he didn't get the Lundquists' fifty thousand dollars."

"No, he didn't," said Kate. "But that also means that we didn't get the Lundquists' little boy back for them."

8 Luck

MAY 4, 8:10 P.M.

The kidnapper thanked his lucky stars for the moving truck. Those cops in the brown van had almost caught up with him. Even with his lights turned off, they probably would have spotted him. But the moving truck had blocked their path just in time.

It was his second stroke of luck that night. His first had come as he was driving up Fifth Street. He had noticed a man in an open black convertible coming toward him. The man had looked familiar. Then, just as he had

reached the phone booth, he had remembered who it was. Lundquist himself! He had
never met him. But he had studied a photo of
the doctor that he had found in a newspaper
in the prison library.

Lundquist was driving a different car! That
meant there was no way the twin car trick
could work. Just as he had realized this and
started to drive off, those hot dog cops had
come after him in their van. If that moving
truck hadn't shown up when it did, he would
be in jail right now.

The thin man drove slowly as he thought
about his next step. He didn't have the
$50,000 now, of course. He couldn't even pay
for the tickets to L.A. And the police would be
looking for this big car. He would have to get
rid of it, steal another car, and leave town.

But first, he had to get the boy. He turned
north toward the motel. He was glad he had
chosen a place in the middle of a whole row
of motels. He had always believed in hiding
things right out in the open. Himself in-
cluded. They didn't call him Slippery for
nothing!

The kidnapper steered the silver sedan

into the parking lot of the Sleepy Daze Motel. He found his favorite spot behind the garbage bin. No point in being too bold.

He got out his keys and hurried to unlock room 2. Inside the dark room, he quietly called the boy's name. Then he reached for the light switch.

Before he could move, a voice broke the silence. "Hold it right there, Slippery. I've got you covered. And my eyes are already used to the dark."

MAY 4, 8:15 P.M.

Kate and Eddy had run the long blocks back to their patrol car. Then they had called in a report over the radio about the florist's van in the fish pond. But they hadn't waited for the tow truck. They still thought they had a chance of tracking down the silver sedan.

Eddy was behind the wheel. "I've had enough of your driving for one night, Brightwater," he said. "I think I'll be able to keep us out of any more goldfish ponds!"

Kate bit back a sharp answer. She knew she had driven as well as anyone could have. But

she also knew Eddy was worried and angry
about losing the kidnapper. She decided to let
him get away with one nasty remark.

"The question is," she said, "where was old
Slippery headed? He must have been hiding
someplace during the past twenty-four hours.
He's got to be keeping Rolfie somewhere. The
boy wasn't in the sedan with him. And speaking of the sedan, where is he hiding it? It's not
an easy car to hide."

"The hotels downtown don't have parking
lots," Eddy thought out loud. "And you have
to pass through a lobby to get to your room.
Lots of people would notice a man with a
scared little boy along."

"That means a friend's house," Kate said.
"Or a motel. Most of them are along the
Washington Pike on motel row."

"We might as well head on up there then,"
Eddy said. "It's better than doing nothing."

He drove the car out of the downtown area
and headed north toward the highway called
the Washington Pike. It was full of motels,
fast-food places, and car dealers. At each
motel they came to, they pulled into the parking lot and drove around slowly, shining their

headlights on the parked cars. There was no
sign of any silver sedan.

After they had passed through the Vacation
Inn lot with no luck, Eddy was about to pull
back onto the highway. But his partner
stopped him.

"Wait a minute," Kate said. "There's one
more dumpy old place right next door to this
one. I think we can get there through that little alley behind this place."

Hall turned the car around. They went back
through the Vacation Inn lot until they came
to the end of the motel. There they found the
alley, and Eddy turned into it.

Bang! The bottom of the police car smacked
down into a huge pothole. Eddy growled and
slowed down. "Great idea of yours, Brightwater. We'll make wonderful speed back here.
Especially if we wreck this car, too!"

Kate started to snap back at him. All at
once, she stopped. She drew in a sharp breath.

"Hall! Look at that!"

Her partner had seen it, too. The headlights
had picked up the dull shine of a car parked at
one side of the alley. It was a large silver
sedan.

Eddy put on the brakes. As quietly as he could, he picked up the car radio. He made a quick report to police headquarters. They would be in touch with the FBI agents who were also out looking for Slippery Jay and the sedan.

Brightwater was already out of the car, quietly moving along the side of the alley. Placing his hand on his gun, Eddy slipped up beside her.

"It's the same car, isn't it, Hall?" she whispered.

"Sure looks like it. But it's hard to tell in the dark. It's a pretty unusual color and make. There can't be many like this in town."

From a few yards away, the police officers tried to make sure the car was empty. The doors were closed. The windows were black. There was no sign of any passengers.

"Let's have a look inside," Kate said at last. Suddenly Eddy's large hand grabbed her arm and squeezed hard. Brightwater stopped short.

Click. The front door of the sedan was beginning to open. At first, it was only a tiny bit. Then, slowly, the opening became larger. As if the door was too heavy for the person inside. Or as if someone was trying to make as little noise as possible.

At the same instant, both Kate and Eddy drew their guns. Then they stood and waited, hoping to take Slippery Jay Judson by surprise.

9 Surprises

MAY 4, 8:25 P.M.

Snap! The lamp in the motel room was switched on. Slippery Jay Judson blinked in the sudden light. He stared at the tall, thin man by the bed. The man's gun was pointed right at him.

Slippery Jay tried a bluff. "What are you doing in my room?" he asked. "Is this a robbery? I don't have any money in here."

The man with the gun smiled. "Come off it, Judson," he said. "Don't play me for a fool. Hand over your gun. And then tell me where the boy is."

Slippery Jay looked quickly around the room. He had been so surprised to find someone waiting for him that he had forgotten all about the boy. His eyes narrowed. He didn't move an inch.

"The gun, Judson!" the man said again. His voice was hard. "Don't try to pretend you haven't got one. I know all your tricks by heart."

Slippery Jay reached into his pocket and pulled out his gun. For a second, he thought of trying to use it. Then he sighed and tossed it onto the bed. This guy had to be some kind of cop. And he had to have his pals outside somewhere. There was no getting away this time. Not even for a man called Slippery.

The tall man stepped forward. Without taking his eyes off Slippery Jay's face, he reached down and picked up the gun on the bed. He stuck it in his belt.

"Now where's the boy, Judson?" he asked again.

Slippery Jay shook his head. "Don't ask *me*," he said. "I left him right here in this room."

The man with the gun looked mad. "Come

off it!" he snapped. "You know you have him stashed somewhere. Unless . . . unless he got in your way and you got rid of him already!"

Now it was Judson's turn to get mad. "Get rid of him!" he cried. "That was my own son! I pulled this whole job for him. They had no right to take him away from me!"

The man with the gun stared at Slippery Jay Judson. Judson really looked upset. He seemed to be telling the truth. But that left the tall man with one big question. What in the world had happened to little Rolfie Lundquist?

MAY 4, 8:30 P.M.

The car door took forever to open all the way. Both Hall and Brightwater were tense, ready to fire. They were expecting to see Judson get out of the silver sedan. Instead they saw a small foot step down onto the street. Seconds later, a little blond boy came around the door and stared at them. They stared back.

Kate and Eddy put away their guns. Slowly Kate stepped forward. She didn't want to scare the child any more. There was no way of knowing what he had been through that day.

"Rolfie?" she asked quietly. "Are you Rolfie Lundquist?"

The little boy didn't say anything at first. He looked scared and puzzled. He stumbled a few steps. His face came into the beam from the police car's headlights. Eddy stared at the boy's eyes.

"Look at those eyes," Eddy said. "I think this kid has been drugged." He bent down and put a large hand on the boy's shoulder. "What's your name, big guy?" he asked.

"It's Rolfie," the boy said. "Can I go home now?"

Kate and Eddy broke into wide grins. They had found the missing child. And he seemed to be all right.

Suddenly they remembered Judson. He could show up at any time. They had to get Rolfie out of the way.

"I'll take him into the squad car," Eddy said. He picked Rolfie up with one arm and started toward the patrol car.

"Right," said Kate. "I'm going to try to find the manager."

Hall and the boy climbed into the squad car while Kate circled around to the front of the motel. Eddy decided to try a few simple questions.

"Where did Toby go, Rolfie?" he asked.

The little boy blinked at him. "Toby?" he said. "Is he here? Can I see him, please?"

"Uh . . . I don't know where he is. What did he do after he brought you here?"

"Toby didn't bring me here," Rolfie said. "I haven't seen Toby all day."

Eddy stared at the child. He wondered if the drug was making Rolfie forget things. But the little boy sounded very sure of himself.

Just then, Kate stuck her head in the car window. She looked as puzzled as Eddy felt.

"The manager's not in his office," she said. "But something strange is going on here."

"You're not kidding," Eddy began. "Rolfie here says . . . "

Kate broke in on him. "There's another car parked behind the garbage bin in the front lot," she said. "As far as I can tell, it looks exactly like this one!"

Eddy stared at Kate. "Two cars," he said slowly. "It might explain a lot of things . . . "

He nodded toward the boy. "But come on in and hear what Rolfie has to say about all this."

Kate climbed into the back seat and listened while Eddy asked the child a few more questions.

"Rolfie, you say Toby the chauffeur didn't bring you here. So who did bring you here?"

The little boy thought hard. "Toby's friend," he said. "But Mommy and Daddy forgot to tell me about him. He's gone now. I was asleep. Then I woke up, and he was gone. I looked out a little window in there and saw our car back here."

"How did you get out here?" Kate asked from behind.

"The window just opened up when I pushed it. I climbed out. And then I fell down. But I didn't even cry!"

"You're a brave kid," said Eddy. "So you pushed open the window and came out. Then you climbed into the car to wait, and you fell asleep? And you didn't see anyone else out here?"

Rolfie started to answer, but suddenly Kate broke in. "Quiet, you two!" she whispered. "Someone's coming!"

Very quietly she pushed open her door and dropped back out onto the alley. With her gun drawn, she waited to see who was coming around from the front of the motel.

10 The Whole Story

The man with the gun jerked his head toward the door of the motel room. "Let's go!" he said.

Slippery Jay was puzzled. He still didn't know who the man was. And he couldn't figure out where the boy had gone. "Where are we going?" he asked.

"I'm taking you in. Now move it, Judson."

The only exit from the room was the door that opened onto the front parking lot. But there was no sign of a police car. To Slippery Jay's surprise, the man ordered him to walk around to the back of the motel. They came out in a small dark alley that ran behind the motel.

Slippery Jay's heart was pounding. He didn't like the looks of this. If this guy was a cop, why was he acting so sneaky? Maybe he was really an old enemy from some past crime. Maybe he just wanted to blow old Slippery away in this dark alley. Well, he wasn't going to go without a fight.

Slippery Jay stopped and turned around. "Listen," he said. "Maybe we could talk this over."

"There's only one thing I want to talk to you about. And that's where the boy is!"

"I tell you, I don't know. But . . ."

"Then keep moving, Judson."

The pair walked a few more yards down the alley. All at once, Slippery Jay gasped. He was looking at a large, silver sedan. It was either the same one he had just parked out front. Or else it was the Lundquists' family car. But what was it doing here?

"How . . . ," he began. "Who . . . "

Just then, the dark alley was flooded with light. A loud voice blasted through the night.

"Toby Thomas! This is the police. You are surrounded. Drop your gun and surrender at once."

Slippery Jay heard the man behind him make a strange sound. He couldn't believe his ears. It sounded almost as if the gunman was laughing to himself!

MAY 4, 8:40 P.M.

Toby Thomas didn't move. He kept his gun trained on the man in front of him. He started to speak. But suddenly something else in the alley moved.

Rolfie had drifted off to sleep again in the police car. Eddy had put him on a blanket on the floor of the back seat where he would be out of the line of fire. The police car door had slid open. A small figure had jumped out and had raced up the alley.

"Toby!" Rolfie screamed. He ran to the chauffeur and wrapped himself around his leg. "Will you take me home? I want Mommy and Daddy!"

The little boy's sobs filled the alley. Kate and Eddy froze. Neither of them knew what to do next. Who was the second man? Why was Toby Thomas holding a gun on him? Most important, how were they going to get Rolfie back?

Kate took a step forward. "Don't touch the boy, Toby," she said. "Put down the gun, and it'll go easier for you."

"You don't understand, Officer," the man began.

"But we do," said Eddy. "You and the boy and the car all disappeared at the same time this morning and . . ."

While everyone else was busy talking, Slippery Jay decided to act. It was now or never. He whirled around and hit Toby's gun hand upward. The gun was knocked free, and a wild shot fired into the night. Toby reacted quickly. But not as fast as Kate. She threw herself forward at Slippery Jay's knees. He crashed to the street. Brightwater jumped on top of his legs, pinning him to the ground. In seconds, Hall was beside her with his gun pointed at the struggling man.

Toby walked toward them. His hand was in his pocket. For one wild moment the cops thought he would pull out another gun. But instead, he took out a wallet and flipped it open to show an ID card.

"FBI!" Kate and Eddy shouted together. Slowly Brightwater got to her feet, pulling her prisoner with her. "Then *this* must be the famous Slippery Jay Judson."

"Right," said Toby. "I'll tell you how I tracked him here—if you tell me how you found Rolfie."

Kate and Eddy smiled. "To tell you the truth," said Hall, "we didn't find him. He found us."

Several long hours later, Hall, Brightwater, and Toby Thomas—whose real name was Brad Claremont—were sitting around a desk at the precinct house. Eddy and Brad were holding steaming cups of black coffee. Kate was drinking carrot juice. Rolfie had been taken home to the happy, sobbing Lundquists. And Slippery Jay Judson was back behind bars.

"You have a lot of questions to answer for us, Brad," Kate was saying. "For one thing, why didn't the FBI let us know you were on the case? We called them in on the Lundquist kidnapping right away. But they never said a word about you."

Brad smiled. "That's easy," he said. "They didn't know where I was. I'd gone completely undercover to look for Judson the day after he escaped from Quincy Prison. No one knew for sure what I was up to. And then today I had no way of getting in touch with our office. Judson had ripped out the phone in the motel room. And I didn't want to leave the place in case he came back while I was away from the room."

"Why don't you just tell us what you did from beginning to end?" Eddy asked. "I think we'll never understand you unless we hear the whole story."

Brad swallowed some coffee and ran a hand over his mouth. "Sure," he said. "When the FBI heard Judson had escaped, they put me on the case. I took the job as the Lundquists' chauffeur because I thought Slippery might be crazy enough to go after his son. At the time of his arrest, he'd talked about some wild dream of his about getting out and taking care of the boy someday. But I didn't want to tell the Lundquists what was going on. I might have been wrong, and it would have scared them for no reason."

He paused and stared at the juice Kate was

drinking. "Do you really like that stuff?" he asked her. Eddy laughed out loud. Kate made a face at both of them.

"Anyway," Brad went on, "this morning I was dressing in my apartment over the garage. I happened to look out the window, and I saw Judson pick up Rolfie in a car that looked exactly like the Lundquists' silver sedan. I don't know if he stole it or bought it or what. But a neighbor stood there and watched them drive off."

"We know," said Kate. "Mrs. Finney. The car fooled her. She thought the Lundquists had hired another new driver."

"There was no time to lose, so I raced down to the garage and jumped into the Lundquists' silver car. I trailed Judson for a while, but I lost him in the morning traffic." Brad drank the last of his coffee. "I spent the rest of the day checking out motels. That big car helped me out there. The Sleepy Daze manager remembered a customer who had one just like it. I hid my car in the alley behind the motel. I didn't want Judson to see it if he came back. Then I went to the manager's office and got the key to room number 2. I sat and waited for Judson."

Eddy scratched his large, square chin. "Hmmm," he said. "We found Rolfie in that car. He must have slipped out the back window after you parked—maybe while you were with the manager. Then he crawled in and went back to sleep. Couldn't help himself with all those drugs he'd been given."

"I guess I just missed him," Brad laughed. "Two ships passing in the night. Anyway, I'm glad you two were on the scene. I don't know how well I could have handled Judson and Rolfie at the same time."

Eddy threw his paper cup into the trash. "Poor kid," he said. "Must have been a rough day for him."

"That's for sure," said Kate. "But it seems Judson didn't really hurt him—except for those drugs. Rolfie still doesn't know that the kidnapper is his father. But the Lundquists are going to tell him the truth before he gets too much older. They've learned they can't hide it from him forever."

"I think he'll handle it OK," said Brad. "I got to know him pretty well while I was working at the Lundquists. He's a tough little guy."

"Well, we'd better get tough now, Hall,"

Kate said. "We haven't even started our reports yet. Remember, three copies of everything!"

Brad said good-bye then and left to go back to FBI headquarters. Kate and Eddy pounded away on their typewriters for a while. Then Eddy yawned loudly. "I'm going to finish this tomorrow," he said. "What about you?"

"Good idea," Kate said. "Let's pack it in. After all, we've been on the go all day—and it's been a long one."

They stood up, pushed in their chairs, and headed for the door. Suddenly Eddy laughed out loud. "It's been a long, hard day all right," he said. "And it's one I'll never forget."

"Why's that, Hall?" asked his partner.

"The first of a lifetime for me, Brightwater. Today was the day I almost arrested an FBI agent!"